For Fairies

Coco Twinkles

MADDY MARA
Author of
Dragon Girls

By Maddy Mara

Forever Fairies

Dragon Girls

Dragon Games

THE SPROUT FAIRIES

Forever Fairies

Coco Twinkles

by Maddy Mara

Scholastic Inc.

ISBN 978-1-339-00121-0

10 9 8 7 6 5 4 3 2 1   24 25 26 27 28

Printed in the U.S.A.   40

First printing 2024

Book design by Cassy Price

It was the middle of the night, and the stars of

the Magic Forest twinkled in the dark velvety sky.

Coco was snuggled in her bed. Suddenly, her nose

twitched. Coco could smell something delicious.

Somewhere, someone was baking!

   She smiled and sat up. It was still so exciting to

remember where she was: in the Sprout Wings branch of the Forever Tree!

Coco looked over at the other three beds in the branch. Lulu, Nova, and Zali, who had sprouted on the same day as Coco, were fast asleep. The four Sprout Wings were quite different, but they had hit it off immediately. Coco just knew that they would be forever friends.

A strange noise filled the room. Coco tilted her head. *Was that thunder? An animal prowling outside?* She grinned. It was Zali, the smallest fairy, snoring!

Maybe that's what woke me up? But Coco was used to Zali's snoring.

No, it was definitely the smell of baking that had pulled her out of a deep sleep. Coco liked every inch of the Forever Tree, but the tree's kitchens were her very favorite. She loved the bustle and excitement. She loved the interesting ingredients. And, of course, she loved the tasty things that were created there.

Quietly, Coco hopped out of bed and grabbed her wand. The Sprouties had been given their wands only a few days ago. But Coco's already felt like it was a part of her.

Sprout Wings were not supposed to leave their branch during the night. But Coco just HAD to find out what that smell was!

The door creaked as she opened it. Coco froze. Hovering near the ceiling was a glow bee, casting a soft, comforting light. It might tell her to go back to bed—but just like Zali, the bee gave a buzzy snore.

Coco crept into the trunk of the tree. The delicious smell grew stronger. But where was it coming from, exactly? Coco didn't think it was the main kitchen, where most fairy meals were made.

I'll let my nose lead the way, she decided.

The tree's curved walls were lined with stairs. Coco tiptoed down, each step emitting a musical note as she descended.

Coco followed the scent for a while, then along

a long, narrow branch. The smell was almost like a hand, beckoning her closer. Finally, she stopped at a little door the color of gingerbread. It was etched with silver-white swirls. In the middle of the swirls was a silver question mark. Coco stared. *What did that mean?*

Opening the door, she found herself in a kitchen. She'd seen the main kitchen a few times. It was always full of fairies from the Twinklestar pod, chatting as they baked and rolled and stirred and sprinkled. Coco loved the way their shiny silver-and-gold outfits were protected by crisp silver aprons.

This kitchen was small and completely silent— except for a low, bubbling sound coming from a brass pot simmering gently on the stove. That must be the source of the delicious smell!

"Hello? Anyone here?" Coco called, fluttering over to the pot.

Inside was a thick mixture of swirling colors. Up close it smelled even yummier—irresistible! Coco reached to dip in her finger . . .

"I wouldn't do that if I were you."

Coco spun around to see a green-faced creature. A troll! Coco and her friends had met a few trolls, but this one was unfamiliar. He had bright green eyes and wavy green hair escaping from a bandanna. A tool belt was slung around his waist, dangling with kitchen implements.

"This is the test kitchen," the troll explained. "Fairies try all kinds of new recipes in here. I wouldn't taste that without knowing what it is. Anything could happen."

Coco grinned. "Really? *Anything?*"

He nodded. "Not so long ago, I became the

first ever blue troll after doing what you were about to do."

Coco clapped her hand over her mouth. "Oh no!"

"Oh yes," said the troll. "The Twinklestars were experimenting with too-blue-berries. I took one sip of the syrup, and I still have a blue tongue."

He stuck out his tongue. It really was blue.

Coco tried hard not to giggle—but it was impossible. "You poor thing!"

The troll shrugged. "It was tasty. I'm Pix, by the way."

"I'm Coco," said Coco, shaking hands. Her hand was half the size of the troll's. "I have a lot of questions. Like, how did you get in here? And even more importantly, *why* are you in here?"

Pix patted a curl of rope attached to his belt. "If we have rope, trolls can get just about anywhere," he said proudly. "As for your second question, I'm here for the same reason you are: tasty things to eat. How about we whip up a snack?"

Coco's wand seemed to shiver with excitement.

But she hesitated, looking at the swirling mixture

again. "What if we get caught? Surely a fairy will

come to check on that pot soon."

"That looks like an overnight recipe to me," Pix

said with a shrug. "C'mon, this is a test kitchen. We're meant to experiment."

Coco considered this. "We might make something really awful."

"We might," Pix agreed, his eyes shining mischievously. "Or we might make the most delicious thing in the whole Magic Forest. Won't know until we try."

This was sounding better and better to Coco. She was itching to cook! She'd often watched the Twinklestars at work as they expertly peeled and sliced and chopped. They kneaded dough and poured batter into tins, ready for the oven. Best of all, the Twinklestars got to sample every tasty thing they made.

"Let's do it!" she said.

Pix began gathering ingredients and placing them on the big wooden table.

"Look, butterfly milk butter," he said, scooping something purple into a bowl. "I've always wanted to try it."

"Ooh! Let's add glow honey!" Coco grabbed a jar and tipped the sparkling liquid into the bowl.

Pix unhooked a strange wooden spoon from his tool belt. It had two scoopy bits instead of one! "I carved it myself," he explained. "Stirs twice as fast.

Hey, this smells good already! See what else you can find."

Coco zoomed around the kitchen, adding a pinch of this and a dollop of that. It was so fun! Every time Pix stirred, the mixture changed color.

"Are you trying out for the Twinklestar pod?" Pix asked as they worked.

"Yes, that's next," said Coco.

So far, she and the other Sprouties had completed two pod tryouts—for Flutterfly and Shimmerbud. The Flutterflies were super fast and agile, and the Shimmerbuds were amazing healers.

Coco had really enjoyed both tryouts. And she'd

done well in both. But she wasn't as fast as Lulu, and she wasn't as good at healing as Nova.

Coco helped stir as she told Pix, "My friend Lulu is amazing at flying. She'll make a perfect Flutterfly. And Nova loves caring for sick and injured creatures. She already feels like a Shimmerbud."

Coco was happy for her friends, she really was. She only wished it was clearer for herself. "The problem is, I'm a mix of things."

Pix looked at her. "That doesn't sound like a problem. The best recipes are a mix of things."

"But I'm a fairy, not a cake!" Coco laughed.

All the same, it was a nice thing for Pix to say. Maybe being a mix *was* a good thing?

Coco noticed some dried flowers hanging from the ceiling. "I think we need one last ingredient. Maybe some of those?"

"Caramel blooms," Pix said. "Great idea."

Coco flew up to pluck two blooms. As soon as she touched them, they broke into sweet-smelling crumbs. Coco sprinkled them into the bowl.

Soon, the mixture frothed and turned a rich yellow.

"Want to try it?" Pix asked. "I don't *think* it will turn your tongue blue."

But before Coco could answer, the door swung open and in walked a whistling Twinklestar fairy. It was Timi, the pod's Alpha Wing. She was tying on an apron, but then she looked up.

Timi gasped. "Coco! What are you doing here?"

Coco was thrilled that the bigger fairy knew her

name. "Hi, Timi! We were testing a recipe. I prom-

ise we'll clean up."

"We?" Timi looked around the kitchen. "Are the other Sprouties here?"

"No, it's just me and—"

But Pix had vanished. A nearby window was slightly ajar.

Timi shook her head. "Let me guess: Pix was here again? I don't really mind—but some mornings we come in and there isn't a single drop of overnight test mixture left! Trolls have excellent taste when it comes to food, so it's a compliment. I thought our too-blue-berry jelly might scare him away, though."

"You did that on purpose?" Coco's eyes were wide.

Timi winked. "Trolls aren't the only ones in this

forest who play tricks. Now, I'm on breakfast duty for you Sprouties. I want to make something extra special. How do you feel about giving me a hand?"

Coco felt very good about it!

"Bowls, please come here," Timi said, beckoning with her wand.

Four large bowls rose from a side bench and floated over. Peeking in, Coco saw they were full of colorful gooey-looking stuff.

She breathed in deeply. "What are we making?"

"A fairy favorite—guessnuts," Timi explained. "The batter is in this pot, and in these bowls are the different fillings. Guessnuts are fiddly to make, but it's worth it. They are so fun to eat. You only know once you've taken a bite what flavor it is!"

Coco couldn't wait!

Timi handed Coco a big shiny ladle. "Scoop up some of the batter, then fling it as high as you can."

Coco loved the sound of this. But she wanted to make sure she had heard right! "Fling it? Won't that make a terrible mess?"

Timi laughed. "That's always a risk. But hopefully my air-frying skills are good enough. Ready?"

Coco plunged the ladle into the mixture and, on the count of three, tossed the batter into the air. Timi drew several quick loops with her wand. There was a burst of light and the batter began to fall—now a perfectly cooked donut!

Timi held out a bowl and caught the donut before it hit the floor. "Well done! Let's make more."

Coco's wand twitched and Timi laughed. "Your wand likes cooking as much as mine does. Some wands hate it."

Together, the two fairies worked until the bowl was full of fresh, warm donuts.

"Can we try one?" begged Coco. "Just to test that they're okay?"

"Not yet," said Timi. "They're missing the best part . . . the filling. Watch!"

Timi took a donut and placed it on the table. Next, she tapped her wand against the side of one of the filling bowls, then drew a squiggly path in the air. A thin cord of goo rose out of the bowl and began wiggling through the air, following her wand toward the donut. When it was directly overhead, it dove into the dough and disappeared.

"Wow!" Coco was impressed. "You would never know there's anything inside."

"That's the fun of guessnuts." Timi grinned. "Here, I'll teach you the filling spell."

Coco loved learning how to send the gooey

mixtures through the air and into the dough. Her wand loved it, too. Soon, there were only a few unfilled donuts left.

"What about these?" Coco asked. "We're out of filling."

"How annoying." Timi sighed. "There isn't time to make more. But hold on—what's in that bowl?"

"That's the mixture Pix and I were making," Coco said. "It's got all kinds of things in it. Butterfly milk butter, caramel flowers, glow honey."

"Sounds delicious." Timi looked impressed. "Let's use it."

"But you haven't tasted it," Coco said, thrilled but a little surprised.

"I *know* it will be yummy. And if it's not"—Timi shrugged as she did the filling spell—"well, that's all part of the fun."

Once all the donuts were magically filled, a large silver tray floated over, already holding a teapot, cups, and sliced fruit. Timi tapped the guessnuts.

Obediently, they bounced onto the platter, which glided toward the door.

"Coco, follow that tray!" Timi cried.

*⁎ ⁎⸱ ⁎⁺

Nova was reading in bed when Coco and Timi arrived. Lulu and Zali were still sleeping.

Nova looked up. "Coco! Where have you been?"

Coco grinned. "Timi and I have been making breakfast. Hungry?"

Lulu sat up. "I am!" She bounded out of bed. "You know me, always starving."

The silver tray floated over to the little table in the center of the room.

"It all looks so elegant!" Zali sighed, stretching.

"Look at the gold trim on those cups."

"And rosebuds on the plates!" Nova added. "I bet food tastes even better when it's eaten off fancy plates."

Timi laughed. "You are the most enthusiastic Sprouties anyone in the Forever Tree can remember. Now, who wants to try a guessnut?"

Coco offered them around before taking a big bite of her own. Honeyed cream, with a hint of lavender, filled her mouth. It was possibly the best thing she'd ever eaten!

She turned to her friends. "What do you think?"

"They're great!" said Lulu. "This red berry filling tastes like magic."

Nova looked surprised. "Berry? Mine is chocolate—and it's very, very yummy."

"Really? Mine is sort of caramelly and buttery," said Zali. Her eyes were enormous. "It's amazing."

"I invented that filling," Coco said proudly. "With the help of a troll called Pix."

Once they realized there were multiple mystery flavors, everyone had to try more. But the Sprouties agreed that Coco and Pix's caramel filling was the best.

"And I was right," Nova declared. "Food *does* taste even better on pretty plates."

Timi smiled. "I have a feeling you four are going to enjoy the Twinklestar tryout."

Of course, the Sprouties had questions about that!

"Do we get to cook something?"

"Is it tomorrow?"

"Will we learn some new spells?"

"Do we get new costumes?"

"So many questions! The answer to the first three is *yes*." Timi waved her wand, and with a pop, four parcels appeared in her lap. "And here's the answer to that last one." She handed a parcel to each fairy.

Excitedly, they ripped them open. Inside each was a silver dress, shaped like a bell; a gold sash; and matching aprons.

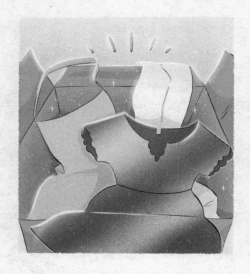

"These are your Twinklestar costumes," said Timi. "They'll adjust to fit you, of course. And feel free to add your own touches to the aprons. Twinklestars love to personalize things."

Zali's face lit up. The little fairy was excellent at crafts. Coco could tell she was already thinking of ways to make her apron unique.

"Can you tell us *anything* about the tryout?" begged Lulu.

Timi smiled mysteriously. "Later. But for now, let's just say you'll need to aim very *high*."

Coco had no idea what that meant, but she had a feeling the Twinklestar tryout was going to be the best one yet!

Timi swished her wand. A whirl of stars streamed through the air, and in an instant, the breakfast dishes were sparklingly clean! With another swish, the plates were neatly stacked on the hovering silver tray. Coco felt her own wand shiver, like it wanted to try out those spells—and she knew how it felt! For Coco, learning spells was one of the best things about being a fairy.

"Right," said Timi. "It's time to visit the Twinklestar branch for a magic lesson!"

As they made their way up the stairs of the Forever Tree, Timi said, "For this tryout, you will be in charge of putting on a high tea."

"What's a high tea?" Zali asked.

"It's very fancy," Timi said. "There are little cakes and scones and tiny sandwiches and tea served in delicate cups. Twinklestars love cooking elaborate things. And our high teas usually have a special twist to them."

"A special twist?" repeated all four Sprouties.

"Well, we always have our high teas in the ball-room," Timi explained. "Up near the chandelier."

"Hold on," said Zali. "There's a ballroom in the Forever Tree? With a chandelier?"

Timi laughed. "Where else would we hold all the fairy balls?"

"Do you mean that everyone flies up to the ceiling with their plates and cups?" asked Lulu.

Timi shook her head. "That would be too easy. No, we make everything float. The tables, the chairs, the teapots, the food. Everything! A high tea tastes even better when you eat it up high."

"So, we have to make everything float up to the judges?" asked Zali. She sounded nervous.

"Not just the judges," Timi said cheerfully. "Everyone in the tree will be there! And because fairies love to dress up, most guests put on their flounce wear. Even the Flutterflies sometimes get out of their flying suits."

Coco knew that the Flutterflies, the fastest fairies, generally didn't like wearing anything that might slow them down. Clearly, a high tea was a big deal.

"So," said Nova in her careful, methodical way, "this tryout is about two things: How our food tastes, and how well we keep everything in the air?"

"Correct!" said Timi. "I know it sounds like a

lot, but don't worry. The Twinklestars will handle the sandwiches and scones and puff cakes. All you need to make is the centerpiece cake. This morning you're going to learn a whole bunch of spells. You'll use them for cooking, of course, but also for the kitchen equipment. And after your lesson, I'll show you how to prepare ingredients for perfectly floaty baking."

Coco bounced on her toes with excitement. This tryout was going to be challenging, but she was so looking forward to it. She gave her wand a little pat. She somehow knew it was as thrilled as she was.

Timi stopped in front of a door covered with

twinkling stars. As the Sprouties watched, one shot across the wooden surface, leaving behind a streak of light.

"How pretty!" said Zali.

"Isn't it?" agreed Timi. "And wait until you see inside!"

As they stepped into the Twinklestar branch, the fairies were surrounded by the inky blue of night-time. Tiny points of light danced in the darkness.

"Ooh!" gasped the Sprouties in wonder.

"The Sprouties are here!" Timi announced. "Stay still, Twinklestars. Give their eyes a chance to adjust."

As Coco's eyes adjusted to the dark, she saw lots

of fairies beaming at them. Twinkling lights shone from their costumes; more were woven through their hair. Even their wands twinkled brightly! Behind the fairies, Coco could see comfy-looking velvet couches, draped with thick, cozy blankets.

"Twinklestars love the dark. And we like to practice magic in the dark," Timi explained. "It helps us stay focused."

Another fairy approached with a handful of glowing lights. "These are for you," she said. She blew gently on the lights, and they rose into the air and came to rest in the Sprouties' hair.

"I love them!" said Zali, shaking her head so the lights twinkled even more.

"I hope we can get them out again," muttered Lulu. "They might slow us down when we fly."

Coco grinned. Lulu was becoming more Flutterfly-ish by the day. Personally, Coco loved how the lights made her long black hair shine!

The Twinklestars gathered around, offering advice about the tryout.

"Don't make your cake too complicated."

"And don't make rock cakes, like I did! They're REALLY hard to float."

"But don't make butterfly cakes, either. Mine tried to fly away."

Timi raised her voice above the chatter. "Okay, everyone, let's take these Sprouties to the kitchen and teach them some of our favorite spells!"

⁺✦ ✳⁺ ⁺✦

"The most important spell is the simplest," began Timi. "The summoning spell. Just remember to be polite. Kitchen utensils do not like rudeness!" She pointed her wand at a wooden spoon. "Two quick swishes back and forth," she said, demonstrating, "then point your wand at the object. You should feel a connection form between them." She made a beckoning gesture with her wand. "Please come here, spoon."

Instantly, the spoon floated over to Timi.

Coco grinned. She couldn't wait to try that!

"And the stir spell," Timi continued, drawing a figure eight with her wand. The spoon stirred in midair. "Not too fast, or you'll make a terrible mess."

The Sprout Wings tried it out, and soon there were four spoons stirring away in front of them.

Coco's spoon stirred at an even, steady rhythm.

Nova's stirring was also good, if a little slow.

Zali's spoon stirred very nicely—but for some reason it was upside down. "Is there something wrong with my wand?"

"You're holding the wrong end," a Twinklestar said gently. She turned Zali's wand up the right way. "It should work a whole lot better now."

Meanwhile, Lulu's spoon was zooming all around, whirling at top speed.

"Your spell is certainly powerful, Lulu," said Timi, ducking as Lulu's spoon whizzed by. "That could come in handy."

Coco smiled. Somehow, the Twinklestars always found something kind to say!

Next, they learned the rise spell, which seemed simple enough but became more complex when used on different objects. The wand action needed to make a chair lift off the ground wasn't quite the same for a piece of cheese, for instance. And making more than one thing rise at the same time was tricky. Each time Coco thought she had everything up, something would either start to drop or shoot up too high.

Lastly, they learned the shaping spell—"To change one tool into another," explained Timi. "Turn a fork into a grater, for instance." She lifted her wand. "Four swishes to the left, four swishes to the right, and imagine the shape you want the object to take."

Lulu turned a fork into a toothpick. Zali changed a silver plate into a heap of glitter. But they all worked it out by the end.

Coco's wand enjoyed all the spells. "Do you some-times feel like your wand is guiding you, rather than the other way around?" she asked the other Sprouties as they worked on the tipping spell (getting water to pour from one glass into another).

"Not really," Lulu admitted.

"Me neither," said Zali, double-checking she was holding her wand correctly.

"I think I know what you mean," Nova said. "It's like you're working *with* your wand, rather than just using it as a tool?"

A nearby fairy leaned over. "That means you've formed strong connections with your wands," she explained. "It's unusual to have that so early."

Finally, Timi clapped her hands and called them over. "Sprouties, you've learned so many spells today! Just remember, being a Twinklestar is about experimenting. Feel free to mix and match to make these spells your own. But now, time for something a little different."

The crowd parted to reveal a fairy holding an enormous basket covered with a golden cloth. Coco could hardly wait to find out what lay beneath it!

With a flourish, Timi whipped the cloth off the

basket to reveal . . .

"Eggs?" Coco asked.

"For now," Timi said. "But there's a Twinklestar

trick that will make them very special indeed.

Come on, we're going into the forest!"

The Sprouties said warm goodbyes to the Twinklestars. Coco was sorry to leave them, but she was curious about this egg trick.

Timi led them downstairs and across the gemstone floor—which shimmered in rainbow colors today—to the Forever Tree's front door.

"Don't forget to change your shoes!" Timi reminded them, the basket of eggs floating alongside her.

As Coco flew out the door, she hovered above the patch of purple moss at the tree's entrance. With a sparkly puff, her slippers changed into little golden shoes, curled at the toe.

Together, the group fluttered into the warm

sunlight. Coco stopped to look up at the Forever Tree. Today it was festooned in tightly folded buds that looked almost—but not quite—ready to burst open.

The Magic Forest was full of activity. As they flew through the trees, Coco saw scampering squirrels, birds flitting from branch to branch, and all kinds of insects hard at work.

Timi pointed out different fruits, nuts, and plants as they flew. "Those yellow berries are sunshine fruits. When you toast them, they make you feel all warm inside. And see those pale pink leaves? They taste a bit minty. Pop some in your apron pockets. You might end up using them tomorrow."

Next, they came across a patch of velvety mushrooms, growing low to the ground.

"These are plushrooms," Timi explained, landing on one and breaking off a piece. A fresh, bread-like smell filled the air. "We slice them very thinly to put in our high tea sandwiches. Also, plushrooms are very fun to bounce on."

Timi demonstrated by jumping from one plushroom to the next. The Sprouties copied her, bouncing high and shrieking as they came whooshing down again.

Finally, Timi leapt off a plushroom and landed neatly on the forest floor. "The soil in this part of the forest tastes exactly like chocolate. Try it."

Lulu, Nova, and Zali stopped bouncing and looked at the dirt doubtfully. But Coco leapt off her plushroom and popped a pinch of the rich-looking earth into her mouth.

"How is it?" asked Zali.

"It tastes like crumbled chocolate!" Coco laughed. "Let's collect some for tomorrow."

The others hopped down and sampled the delicious chocolatey soil.

They continued through the forest, their pockets soon bulging with berries, nuts, soil, flowers, and leaves.

Finally, Timi stopped flying and hovered in mid-air. She stretched out her arms.

"Here we are! At the Rainbow Glade!"

"Why's it called that?" asked Nova, looking around the lovely meadow. "Is it because of the different-colored flowers?"

"Good theory," said Timi. "But no. Wait and see."

The clouds above cleared and sunlight began pouring into the glade. But it wasn't ordinary light—it was striped with every color of the . . .

Lulu gasped. "Rainbow! A rainbow is forming!"

Timi nodded. "This is the most reliable rainbow in the forest. It has formed here, at the same time every day, for as long as any fairy can remember. And the best bit? When you roll eggs down this rainbow, they become extra light and fluffy."

"Amazing!" said Coco.

"Won't they break when they hit the ground?" Nova asked. Coco was eager to try rolling eggs, but she loved how careful Nova always was.

"Not if we make a pile of petals for them to land in." Timi pointed. "Let's pick those big white flowers over there. Afterward, we'll grind them up for flower-flour. Flower-flour makes the lightest cakes."

As the Sprouties gathered armfuls of petals, Coco couldn't resist touching the rainbow. It was warm and slightly spongy.

"Time to roll!" announced Timi. She whooshed into the air, the basket of eggs following close behind.

Coco, Lulu, Nova and Zali zoomed off after Timi and the eggs. Coco loved the feeling of air streaming through her hair as they flew higher. The group followed the curve of the rainbow until they burst through the canopy of trees. The Magic Forest stretched as far as Coco could see, like a vast green ocean.

Timi pulled an egg from the hovering basket. "I'll roll the first one so you can watch." She carefully placed the egg on the highest point of the rainbow and let go. It rolled down the arch, picking up speed, then disappeared out of view.

"Are you sure it won't break?" Zali clasped her hands anxiously.

"I promise it won't!" Timi said. "When you've each sent one down, there will be five fluffified eggs waiting in our petal pile."

Coco went first, followed by Lulu, then Zali. For a heart-stopping moment, it looked like Zali's egg was going to topple off the edge! But it corrected itself and rolled merrily away. Finally, Nova's egg rolled slowly and precisely down the very center of the rainbow.

"Good rolling, everyone," said Timi. "Let's go get our eggs!"

Lulu led the way, and the fairies whooped and twirled as they zoomed back through the treetops.

"I hope we don't find smashed eggs at the end of the rainbow!" said Nova.

When the group landed, they did not find smashed eggs. They did not find any eggs at all.

"They've vanished!" exclaimed Lulu.

"Maybe an animal came along and ate them?" suggested Nova.

"Or they rolled into a burrow?" said Zali.

"Hmm, shall we roll some more?" Coco asked Timi.

Timi shook her head. "It's too late. The rainbow is fading."

Sure enough, only the faintest glimmer of the rainbow remained. The fairies looked at one another in dismay.

There was strange clanking sound from the thicket. Coco tilted her head. The noise was familiar somehow.

Timi crossed her arms and faced the dense bushes. "Come out, Pix! I know you're there!"

Pix emerged, his kitchen tools clinking and clank-ing as he pushed through the bushes. He carried a sturdy backpack and a coil of rope. "Hey, Timi, hey, Sprout Wings," he said casually. "What's up?"

Timi raised an eyebrow. "Pix, did you take our rainbow-rolled eggs?"

"Eggs?" Pix repeated. "Rolled down a rainbow, you say? What an interesting technique! I bet that makes them extremely fluffy and delicious. Sorry, haven't seen them."

Coco liked Pix, she really did. But she was pretty sure he was lying to Timi.

She stepped forward. "Pix, you know that mixture we made together? We used it in our breakfast guessnuts. And guess what? It was delicious!"

"It really was," Zali piped up.

Pix looked pleased. "We made a good team, Coco. We should cook again some time."

"I'd like that," said Coco slowly. "But first, the Sprouties all have to get through the Twinklestar tryout. And for that, we need those eggs."

Pix scratched his chin. "Come to think of it, I might have picked up some eggs. And actually, they *were* just here at the base of the reliable rainbow."

Coco and Timi exchanged a glance.

Pix rummaged in his bag. He pulled out strips of bark, strange-looking seed pods, lumpy roots covered in dirt. Lastly, he carefully removed some eggs.

"Thanks," Coco said, returning them to the basket. *All's well that ends well*, she thought. So why did she still feel like something was wrong?

"Good luck with the tryout!" Pix said, then disappeared into the dense forest.

"Trolls," Timi tutted. "Coco, you handled that well. Come on, Sprouties. Let's get back."

As they began zooming home, Timi asked the Sprout Wings a big question.

"Do any of you know which pod you'd like to be in?"

"Flutterfly!" called Lulu, doing a midair loop.

Coco thought about the Flutterfly pod. They used their fast-flying skills to help everyone in the forest. If a creature needed rescuing, the Flutterflies were always there first. That would be so exciting.

"For me, it's Shimmerbud," Nova said. "I just love making potions and healing the forest's creatures."

In the Shimmerbud tryout, they had made a

potion to cure the snufflebugs. That was wonderful. She knew that being a Shimmerbud would be very rewarding.

But Coco was also looking forward to the Twinklestar tryout! Why was it so difficult to choose a favorite pod?

"I haven't decided yet," Zali admitted.

"Me either! In fact, I kind of want to be in all of them," said Coco.

"I was the same," Timi said. "I liked flying fast, and I liked working in the hospital burrow. And I really enjoy arts and crafts. But in the end, it was cooking that I *loved*. Speaking of which, any ideas for your cake?"

"So many!" Coco laughed. "How many flavors can one cake have?"

"As many as you like." Timi looked surprised by the question. "As far as Twinklestars are concerned, there is no such thing as too much. Especially when it comes to cake! We like cakes that are big and bold and interesting. Even weird flavors can be delicious, don't you think?"

The others looked a little doubtful, but Coco nodded enthusiastically.

As the Forever Tree loomed ahead, Timi gave them another piece of good news. "You all get free time this afternoon. Remember, you're going to need a lot of energy tomorrow."

⁺ *⁺*⁺ *⁺*

Back in the tree, the Sprouties parted ways. Coco knew what each would be doing. Lulu would go outside to work on her spins and twirls. Nova would visit the patients in the hospital burrow. And Zali would no doubt be in the craft branch, making something fabulous.

As for Coco, she raced down to the test kitchen. She wanted to make a snack, then work on ideas for their cake.

It has to be something that no one has done before, she decided. *Something with all the flavors of the forest in it.*

Ideas swirled around Coco's head as she nibbled

on crackers and pink-swirl dip. But it wasn't until much later, when the Sprouties were tucked into their cozy beds, that Coco landed upon the perfect idea.

She sat bolt upright. "Sprouties!" she whispered. "Want to hear my cake idea?"

But the room was completely silent. Except, of course, for the sound of Zali's snores.

"Wake up, wake up! It's tryout day!"

Coco blinked open her eyes. Timi was standing in the middle of the Sprout Wings branch, already wearing her apron and her usual broad smile.

"Too early," mumbled Zali from under her pink lily coverlet. "It's still dark outside."

"Sure is. The Twinklestar tryout always starts at dawn!" Timi replied cheerily. "Get ready quickly and I'll take you to the kitchen."

Coco leapt out of bed. Getting up early to cook was easy!

Nova stretched and sat up, pulling her dark curls into a bun.

"What about breakfast?" asked Lulu, hungry as always.

"There will be food galore, I promise," said Timi.

Lulu leapt out of bed. "Hey, has anyone seen my apron? It's vanished."

"Mine too," said Nova.

Coco saw that her apron was also missing. How strange!

"I've got them all," said Zali, pulling a parcel out from under her bed. "I thought I'd make them extra special."

The little fairy handed out the aprons, her cheeks pink with excitement. Coco unfolded hers to see that Zali had carefully painted a swirly red *C* onto hers. Nova's apron had a purple *N*, and Lulu's had a yellow *L*. Each letter had a little pair of wings sprouting from it.

"I painted them in your sprout flower colors," explained Zali, showing them hers, with a pink *Z*.

Coco, Nova, and Lulu hugged Zali.

"These aprons are definitely going to help us *fly* through the tryout!" Coco said.

Before long, all four Sprouties were washed and dressed in their Twinklestar outfits. They hurried up the musical stairs behind Timi.

Coco gazed down. "Look! The gemstone floor is the Twinklestar colors." This gave Coco a burst of energy. "Oh! That reminds me: Last night I was thinking about what cake we should make. What do you guys think?"

"We should make something with lots and lots of chocolate," said Lulu.

"Maybe something light and fluffy would be better?" suggested Nova. "It needs to float, remember."

"I vote for fruit-flavored," said Zali. "We collected so many delicious berries in the Magic Forest yesterday."

"All great ideas," Timi said.

"That's lucky." Coco grinned. "Because here's my

idea: We do them all! I was thinking we should make a layered cake, each a different flavor. One layer for each of us."

"Four layers would be amazing!" said Nova. "But won't that make our cake really heavy?"

"We have rainbow-rolled eggs, remember," said Coco. "Plus all the new spells we learned."

The musical stairs led them up and up the main trunk. Coco was puzzled. They were almost at the top of the staircase. They'd never been so high! Where were they going? When they finally reached the top, Timi tapped the roof with her wand. A trapdoor appeared, and when Timi opened it, Coco saw *another* staircase.

"There are more rooms up here?" she asked, amazed.

"Oh yes!" Timi laughed. "Come on, I'll show you."

The Sprouties kept climbing until they reached a little silver door.

"Welcome to the under-kitchen," announced Timi, swinging it open.

The sound of merry voices and clanking pans greeted the fairies.

"Why is it called the under-kitchen?" asked Nova.

"Yes, when it's so high in the tree?" added Lulu.

But before Timi could explain, the Sprouties were surrounded by Twinklestars, all holding platters of food.

"Come in, little Sprouties!" called the older fairies.

"Good to see you again!"

"We're just finishing the other treats for your high tea!"

The Sprouties were led to a huge workbench in the middle of the kitchen.

"Want crunch buns for breakfast? They're fresh out of the oven." A fairy with a gold swirl painted on her apron produced a plate and put four buns on it.

"Try these mini hummingbird egg and lilac leaf sandwiches!" said another fairy, adding four sandwiches to the plate.

"Oh, you HAVE to have our rainberry drop cakes," insisted yet another Twinklestar.

Nova laughed. "We can't eat all of this!"

"Don't listen to Nova." Lulu mock-glared at her friend and grabbed a bun. "Of course we can."

"Try a few things," said Timi. "You'll need your strength before we meet the Forever Wings in the ballroom."

Coco's excitement grew. The Forever Wings were the elders of the tree. They judged the tryouts and decided which fairy belonged in which pod. They were very grand and important!

Coco took a nibble of a hummingbird egg sandwich. The bread was light and airy, and the filling was fresh and a little salty. Delicious! "Where is the ballroom?" she asked. She had a sudden image of trying to make their four-layered cake float up staircases and along corridors.

"Not far. In fact, it's above us." Timi laughed at their puzzled expressions. "Watch."

The Alpha made a grand gesture with her wand, and the kitchen's roof opened to reveal ... the ballroom!

"It's so beautiful!" whispered Zali, gazing up.

The ballroom's domed ceiling was a painted sky, complete with fluffy clouds and brightly colored birds. Dangling from the ceiling was the famous chandelier. It was as big as a hundred fairies and shone like a thousand moonbeams.

Fairies flitted about, chatting happily as they strung up decorations and herded bobbing cushions into place around hovering tables. Floating in the middle of it all, on four ornate chairs, sat the Forever Wings.

Coco turned to Timi, her eyes bright. "It's amazing!"

"Isn't it?" agreed Timi. "The under-kitchen and ballroom were created together. When high tea is ready, the goodies can float right up."

The Sprouties grinned at one another. The Flutterfly and Shimmerbud tryouts had been challenging and fun. But the Twinklestar tryout was going to be grand and—hopefully—delicious!

Coco was already imagining the gasps of amazement and delight when their layered cake slowly rose into the ballroom.

"Okay," said Timi. "Time to speak to the Forever Wings."

The friends helped one another clean up. Lulu

brushed away the icing on Zali's cheek, and Nova pulled out a blob of sparkleberry jelly from Coco's hair.

"Ready?" Coco asked. She knew the others got nervous when speaking to important fairies. But Coco loved being near the elders, and her wand twitched with excitement. These fairies were very powerful, but they were always kind.

"Ready!" called Lulu, Nova, and Zali together.

They flew through the open roof and lined up in front of the judges, holding hands in a row.

The elders all smiled, but it was the Twinklestar elder in her gorgeous silver-and-gold gown who spoke.

"Hello, Sprout Wings. As you know, today you four must make a cake for the tree's high tea. Forever Fairies love a high tea, and the Twinklestars are the tree's bakers."

The Flutterfly elder's eyes sparkled mischievously. "If you're looking for a Twinklestar, the chances are you'll find them in one of the kitchens. Often covered in flower-flour!"

"It's true." The Twinklestar elder chuckled. "Today's tryout requires a mix of clever cooking and imaginative spells. When we taste-test your cake, we will be judging it on its flavor, texture, and appearance. But we'll also be judging the spells you use to make it rise—and stay afloat."

Coco took a deep breath. It was a lot! But she was certain they could do it.

"One last thing," added the elder. "Your cake must be ready in one turn of the Glitter Clock." With a flick of her wand, she made a winged hourglass appear. Its two connected bulbs were filled with silver-and-gold glitter. "No one likes a tree full of hungry fairies!"

Coco glanced at her friends. They all looked rather worried. It was up to her to reassure them. "We can't wait to get going," she declared.

"Wonderful!" The air seemed to buzz as the Twinklestar elder raised her wand and swished it once more through the air, releasing tiny silver-and-gold stars. They swirled around the Glitter Clock, which flipped over, its little wings fluttering madly. "Then I officially declare: The Twinklestar tryout has begun!"

8

The Sprout Wings zoomed to the under-kitchen, followed closely by the Glitter Clock. Lulu led the way, as always, but Coco wasn't far behind. She felt like her excitement had given her an extra pair of wings!

Timi flew with them. As they landed, the roof

closed overhead. "I can't help you during the tryout, of course," Timi said, "but you have every-thing you gathered in the forest and the spells we learned yesterday. When your time is up, the roof will open. The treats we've made will rise. And if everything goes well, your cake will, too!"

"There's nothing as exciting as a cake launch," a nearby Twinklestar sighed, putting the final touches on a tray of scones.

"Good luck, Sprouties!" called the other Twinklestars cheerfully as they flew out of the kitchen.

"Don't worry. Just cook the most delicious, most original cake any of us have ever tasted!"

"Then make it float! Easy!"

"Sooooo easy," said Lulu, rolling her eyes but laughing.

"It's going to be difficult," said Nova. "But I think we can do it."

"We can definitely do it," Zali said firmly. "Thanks to Coco, we've got a great cake idea. Plus, we have great ingredients. And best of all, we're a great team."

Coco gave the little fairy a hug, then looked around the kitchen. Like the other fairy kitchens, there was a huge and spotlessly clean oven, and the walls were lined with shelves. These were piled high with bowls, saucepans, spoons, and cake tins in every possible shape and size.

"Which cake layer should we make first?" Nova asked.

"Maybe we should make them all at once?" Coco suggested. "That oven could easily fit all four tins, and we'll be quicker that way. We only have one turn of the Glitter Clock, after all."

"Plus, something might go wrong," Lulu added.

"Nothing will go wrong," Coco said. "Let's find some big mixing bowls."

"Over there." Zali pointed. "They look heavy."

"We can use the summoning spell!" Coco reminded them.

Coco swished her wand in the way they'd been taught, feeling the bond form between her wand

and the bowls. "Mixing bowls, would you mind coming to help us?"

Instantly, four big brass bowls floated over to the workbench.

"It worked!" Zali cried.

"Don't look so surprised." Coco laughed.

Soon the Sprouties were hard at work. Into each mixing bowl they put flower-flour, glow honey, and butterfly milk butter. Coco cracked an egg into one of the bowls.

"Can you tell it was rainbow-rolled?" asked Lulu, peering over her shoulder.

"Nope. It looks like a normal egg." Coco felt a tiny bit disappointed. She'd hoped for rainbow yolks. *The most important thing is that they work,* she told herself.

Next, the fairies pulled out their special ingredients.

"Lots of chocolate dirt for this layer!" Lulu tipped the magical soil into the first bowl.

"Cloudberries for this layer," said Zali, sprinkling them into the next.

"Now, for the light-as-a-feather float flowers." Nova crumbled the sweet-smelling blossoms into the third bowl.

"Minty leaves and spice-bark for the last layer," Coco sang, "and it's time to stir!" She politely summoned over some big wooden spoons, which jumped eagerly into the batter.

"Can I do the stirring spell?" begged Lulu.

"Sure," said Coco.

Lulu swished her wand and all four spoons began to stir enthusiastically. Lulu zoomed over and grabbed one spoon handle, whizzing around in giant circles.

"Wheeee!" she called as she spun around and around. "This is fun!"

"I've got to try that," said Zali, grabbing hold of the spoon that was stirring the berry mixture.

"Me too," Nova said.

There was no way Coco was going to miss out! Soon all four fairies were whizzing around in circles, squealing with laughter.

Finally, the spoons slowed to a stop and the fairies let go.

"I'm soooo dizzy!" Zali giggled, flying in a very wonky line back to her spot at the bench.

"Same," Lulu said. "That was so fun! Can we do it again?"

Coco looked at the hourglass. About a third of the glitter had already settled in the lower bulb. She shook her head regretfully. "We don't have time. Besides, too much beating isn't good for cakes. Let's get them into the oven."

"Which tins should we use?" Nova asked.

"The stars!" chorused Coco, Lulu, and Zali.

Coco politely summoned four enormous star-shaped tins, and Nova performed a tipping spell, transferring the batter into each. She didn't spill a drop! Finally, Coco sent them into the oven.

She checked the time again. "When the glitter is exactly halfway, we'll take out the cakes," Coco told the others.

"Shall we make the frosting while we wait?" Nova suggested.

"Ooh, yes!" Zali clapped.

Coco nodded. "I spotted some dried cloud dust." She pointed to a cupboard of supplies. "And there's a bottle of liquid forest air there. Maybe we could make a kind of cloud fluff mixture?"

"Sounds great," said Lulu, rubbing her tummy. "Do you have a recipe?"

"No," admitted Coco. "Let's just make it up as we go."

Coco tipped the cloud dust into a fresh bowl. Lulu poured in the liquid air, and the mix puffed up, becoming light and fluffy and smelling of warm summer days. Coco summoned a tall metal spoon to help stir, and the fairies took turns holding on. It went even faster than the wooden spoons!

As they worked, the kitchen filled with the delicious smell of baking. At the Glitter Clock's halfway point, they got the cakes out.

"I want to try them right now," groaned Lulu.

"How can we tell if they're going to float?" Nova wondered.

"Should we try a rising spell on them?" Zali said.

Coco hesitated. "Let's add a first coat of frosting and then check if the spell works before we decorate?" she suggested.

The Sprouties removed the cakes from their

tins, slathered them with cloud fluff frosting, and carefully stacked them vertically. The star points of the layered cake twitched, as if it were ready to fly.

"It already looks fantastic!" Coco cried. "Let's do the rise spell together."

But just as the Sprout Wings pulled out their wands, the kitchen door flung open. Pix the troll rushed in, a strange look on his face.

"Coco! There's something I need to tell you," he cried.

"Not right now, Pix," Coco said. "We're about to test our cake!"

Coco, Lulu, Nova, and Zali swirled their wands.

To everyone's delight, the huge star cake quivered and lifted into the air.

"It's working!" squealed Zali, jumping up and down as the cake floated higher still.

"Coco, this is important," said Pix, sounding stressed. "It's about the—"

The enormous cake gave a shiver, plummeted to the ground, and splattered everywhere.

The Sprouties gasped. "Nooooooo!"

It was a total disaster. Four flavors of cake were strewn all over the kitchen. The fairies themselves were covered in blobs of frosting and chunks of warm cake.

Coco couldn't believe it. Their creation was

ruined. She looked at the Glitter Clock. Time was nearly up!

For the first time since she'd sprouted, Coco felt a wave of doubt. *What happens if we fail the tryout?* Even worse—this was all her fault. Was her idea of four layers too much?

"Coco?"

She jumped. She was so lost in thought, she hadn't heard Pix approach.

"Coco, I'm so sorry."

She shook her head. "It's not your fault, Pix. I clearly did something wrong." All her energy and enthusiasm was seeping away. "I guess this means I'm not cut out to be a Twinklestar." Coco realized,

suddenly, how much she wanted to be in the Twinklestar pod.

"Listen to me!" Pix cried. "This is not your fault. It's mine!"

Coco frowned. "What are you talking about?"

Without a word, Pix opened his backpack and pulled out an egg, then neatly cracked it open.

The Sprouties leaned in to look.

"A rainbow yolk!" said Zali. "What kind of egg is that?"

Coco gasped. "Oh, Pix."

"That's a rainbow-rolled egg, isn't it?" said Nova, clearly understanding, too.

Pix nodded sadly. "I swapped them for the ordinary eggs I had in my bag."

"Why would you do that?" asked Coco.

Pix kicked at the ground, looking uncomfortable. "I wanted to try your fancy cake," he admitted.

"I've always longed to come to a fairy high tea, but I've never been able to because I can't fly. I thought I'd stop your cake from floating so I could taste it." Big green tears rolled down his cheeks. "I didn't know that it would smash like that. I'm sorry! You have to believe me!"

Coco sighed. She believed that Pix hadn't meant to ruin their cake. He just loved trying delicious new things.

"What do we do?" asked Lulu. "Our time is nearly up."

Coco looked at her friends. Their wings drooped with disappointment. The cake was ruined, and they didn't have time to make another.

Then she looked at all the smashed bits of cake. It was mostly chocolatey brown, with little slivers of minty leaves and bright berries here and there.

"There's NO WAY we are giving up," Coco said.

Nova and Lulu brightened.

Zali gave Coco a hug. "I knew you'd have an idea!"

In fact, Coco only had half an idea. But perhaps that was enough. "Our broken cake looks like the base of the Forever Tree," she said slowly, her half idea beginning to unfurl in her mind. "Maybe instead of trying to make our cake float, we could make it *grow*? And instead of a star-shaped cake, we make one that looks like the Forever Tree!"

Everyone started talking at once.

"That's a great idea! I bet the elders have never eaten a tree-cake before," Zali said.

"What spells could we use?" asked Lulu.

"The rise spell," said Nova.

"And maybe the bloom spell?" suggested Zali.

Coco nodded. These would definitely be useful. But they needed something else.

"I've got it!" she cried. "The shaping spell!"

Nova nodded thoughtfully. "It's a hard spell. But it's worth a try."

Zali smiled. "Let's do it together."

"And let's do it soon!" urged Lulu, looking at the clock.

Coco pulled out her wand. "Everyone remember how?"

"Four swishes to the left," said Lulu.

"And four to the right," continued Zali.

"And think about the form you want the object to become," finished Nova.

Together, the friends swirled their wands to the left, then to the right. Coco closed her eyes and pictured the Forever Tree. Its wide trunk, its rough, protective bark. The strong, gracious branches and bright, lush leaves. Finally, abundant flowers blooming. The image was so clear in Coco's head she could almost hear the rustling leaves.

Hang on. She COULD hear the rustling leaves!

Coco opened her eyes. There, growing in front of her, was a mini Forever Tree. Made from cake!

"It's working!" Zali squealed.

"And it's perfect," Nova whispered. "Just *way* too small."

"Shall we use the rise spell again?" suggested Lulu.

Pix, who had been watching all this silently, stepped forward. "I have some troll tech that might help." He pulled out a strange-looking contraption. "This is a troll puffer. Trolls can't rainbow-roll eggs, so we use these. It won't make your cake lift off the ground, but it will make it lighter and puffier."

Coco beamed. "That's perfect, Pix! If it's a

tree-cake, it should stay rooted to the ground—like a real tree. But we also need it to reach toward the sky. Or in this case, the chandelier in the ballroom."

Pix's eyes brightened. "Try this, too." He waved a gnarled root in the air. "It's from the light plant. They're famous for growing toward the light. It also tastes delicious. Maybe grate some onto your cake?"

Coco dusted light root shavings over the branches and leaves, and their tree-cake gave a little shake.

"The glitter has almost all run out!" Lulu warned.

"Quick, let's use Pix's troll puffer!" said Coco.

They set to work. Pix stuck the puffer into the

trunk of the tree-cake, and let the fairies take over. Lulu and Zali took turns to jump up and down on it to make the air whoosh in. The cake began to grow bigger, and bigger, and taller! At the same time, Nova did another rise spell, and Coco continued with the shaping spell, making sure the cake kept growing like a tree.

"It's working!" cried Zali as she jumped on the puffer.

The tree-cake reached toward the ceiling and Coco's hope grew along with it. Maybe, just maybe, they would pass this tryout after all!

10

The door to the under-kitchen swung open again and Timi entered, the lights in her hair twinkling brightly. When she saw the rapidly growing tree-cake, her eyes twinkled, too. "I came to check if you were ready. Clearly you are!"

The Glitter Clock had wound down, and the ceiling folded open.

The ballroom was now full of fluttering fairies, dressed in their finest flounce wear. The Twinklestars had all taken off their aprons and wore lights in their hair. Everyone looked down at the still-growing tree-cake.

Gasps filled the huge space.

"Oooooooooh!"

"Is that a tree-cake?"

"I've never seen anything like it!"

The ballroom looked even more beautiful now. Lacy tablecloths covered the gently bobbing tables, and steaming teapots floated near the walls. Coco spotted the judges floating high on their chairs, now with a little table in front of them. In the middle of everything glowed the chandelier.

Coco looked closely. Had it changed shape? With a laugh, she realized the chandelier was made of crystal raindrops and a huge cluster of glow bees! As she watched, they moved into a different formation.

The air buzzed—with the sound of glow bees and anticipation!

"Let's add a finishing touch," Zali suggested, holding up a pouch. "Edible glitter!"

"Great idea," said Coco.

The fairies grabbed handfuls of golden sparkles. They flew around the tree-cake's twisting branches, sprinkling as they went. Coco breathed in the rich, chocolatey aroma. Would their cake taste as good as it looked? In her excitement, she accidentally sprinkled some of the glitter on herself.

"Coco, you're twinkling!" Nova laughed.

Coco grinned. "I'm twinkling on the inside, too."

The tree-cake seemed to be growing even faster now. It stretched up and up toward the shimmering chandelier.

The watching fairies oohed and ahhed with delight. Just as the topmost cake branches neared the Forever Wings' table, the tree-cake stopped growing, and there was a moment of silence.

Then the ballroom erupted into wing-fluttering,

clapping, and cheering. The Twinklestar elder raised her wand, and finally the crowd quieted.

"Well done, Sprout Wings," she said. "This is a *very* impressive high tea cake. How in fairydom did you come up with such an idea?"

"Well, our first cake was kind of a mess,"

admitted Coco. "So we had to make something new, very quickly."

The elder nodded sagely. "Big messes often lead to new ideas. I think it's wonderful that you've thought to make a cake that is both low and high. And I see some trolls want to join in our celebration."

Way down below, Coco spotted not just Pix but also other trolls! Lex, Rox, and Tex waved up at the fairies.

"I invited some friends," Pix called. "You know that trolls are the best judges of fairy food. And we're honest—we never pretend to like something."

The Forever Wings roared with laughter at this.

"Very true," said the Twinklestar elder. "There's a fairy saying: Troll praise is the highest praise. Now, perhaps you can give us a slice of your cake?"

The Sprouties politely summoned knives, cake forks, and golden plates. They cut a slice for each of the Forever Wings, taking care to make them looked as pretty as possible.

Coco's heart fluttered as she sent the plates over to the judges. She knew their cake looked impressive, but how would it *taste*?

The moment the elders took their first bites, it

was clear that there was nothing to worry about. They smiled and nodded at one another, mouths too full to speak.

"Tell me," said the Twinklestar elder when she'd swallowed her mouthful, "how did you feel making this cake?"

Coco looked at her friends. It had *not* been fun when the cake smashed. But that was only one moment of the whole experience. The rest of it had been so much fun! Just thinking about holding on to those whizzing, stirring spoons made Coco want to make another cake. Perhaps Twinklestar really was the pod for her?

"We loved it!" the Sprouties cried as one.

"I can tell," said the Twinklestar elder. "I can taste the flavors of the Magic Forest, but there's also a lightness that only comes when the bakers are having fun. Congratulations, Sprout Wings. You have passed the Twinklestar tryout!"

As a roar erupted throughout the ballroom, Coco felt her wand twitch. A new symbol was magically appearing: a tiny twinkling star.

Pix's loud voice boomed out from below. "When can we try the cake? We can't wait much longer!"

The elders laughed.

The Twinklestar elder raised her wand into the air. "Let the first ever high-low tea begin!" She swished her wand and the trays of goodies made by the Twinklestars began moving from guest to guest. Silver knives began expertly cutting the cake, flipping slices onto waiting plates. The plates darted off to hungry fairies . . . and even hungrier trolls.

"What do you think, Pix?" Coco asked, fluttering down to where the trolls were feasting by the foot of the tree-cake.

"It's . . . well, it's perfect." Pix grinned.

The other trolls gave the thumbs-up, their green cheeks bulging with cake.

Coco beamed. Truly, Pix's opinion mattered as much as the judges'.

Once everyone had tasted everything, the

Sprouties were called back to the Forever Wings' table. This time, the elder dressed in dusty pink and aqua addressed them. "Your final tryout is for my pod. Are you ready to learn all about the Sparkleberries?"

Coco pulled her friends into a hug. Of course they were ready!

Turn the page for a special sneak

peek of Zali's fairy adventure!

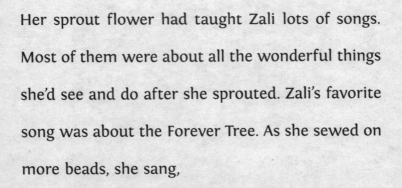

Her sprout flower had taught Zali lots of songs. Most of them were about all the wonderful things she'd see and do after she sprouted. Zali's favorite song was about the Forever Tree. As she sewed on more beads, she sang,

Do you know the Forever Tree?

Growing here for eternity.

Standing tall for all to see

It's the—

Zali stopped singing as the door suddenly flung open. Standing there was the most extraordinary creature Zali had ever seen. Was she a troll? She was mostly green. But unlike the other trolls Zali had met, her hair was bright pink. So were her fingernails. And she wasn't wearing the sturdy work clothes that most trolls wore. This troll was swathed in shimmering fabric, and around her neck was a huge, twinkling necklace. Instead of clompy troll boots, she wore gold slippers.

While Zali stared, the unexpected visitor finished Zali's song in a deep, rich (and not quite in tune) voice.

"It's the home of you and me!"

Zali was usually shy when meeting someone for the first time, but she was too surprised to be shy. She was also too surprised to speak!

"I know what you're thinking," said the troll, sweeping into the room. "I'm far too glamorous to be a troll. But troll I am, and proud of it." She sat beside Zali. "My name is Hux. And I want to learn how to sew. Tell me, little fairy with the sweet voice and the sewing needle in her hand, will you teach me?"

ABOUT THE AUTHORS

Maddy Mara is the pen name of Australian creative duo Hilary Rogers and Meredith Badger. Hilary and Meredith have been making children's books together for many years, including the Forever Fairies, Dragon Games, and Dragon Girls series. They love dreaming up new ideas and always have lots of projects bubbling away. When not writing, Hilary can be found cooking weird things or going on long walks; she would be half Twinklestar and half Shimmerbud if she was a Forever Fairy. And Meredith can be found teaching English online all around the world or daydreaming about being able to fly; she'd be a Shimmerbud if she were a Forever Fairy. They both currently live in Melbourne, Australia. Find out more at maddymara.com.

THE SPROUT FAIRIES

Forever Fairies

Forever fairies . . . and forever friends!

READ THEM ALL!

DRAGON GIRLS

**#1: Azmina the Gold
Glitter Dragon**

**#2: Willa the Silver
Glitter Dragon**

**#3: Naomi the Rainbow
Glitter Dragon**

**#4: Mei the Ruby
Treasure Dragon**

**#5: Aisha the Sapphire
Treasure Dragon**

**#6: Quinn the Jade
Treasure Dragon**

**#7: Rosie the
Twilight Dragon**

**#8: Phoebe the
Moonlight Dragon**

**#9: Stella the
Starlight Dragon**

**#10: Grace the
Cove Dragon**

**#11: Zoe the
Beach Dragon**

**#12: Sofia the
Lagoon Dragon**

Collect them all!

DRAGON GAMES

PLAY THE GAME. SAVE THE REALM.

READ ALL OF TEAM DRAGON'S ADVENTURES!